# THE WORLD OF

# PETER RABBIT™

## Sticker Activity Book

# Christmas Sticker Fun!

Use your **STICKERS** to decorate this page!

Based on the books by
## BEATRIX POTTER

# A Snowy Sticker Scene

The first snow has fallen and all the animals are busy gathering decorations for their homes this Christmas. Stick the bunnies and their friends in the scene, and fill their baskets with pine cones, berries and leaves.

# Peter's Advent Calendar

Peter and his sisters can't wait to open their advent calendar every day of December. Match stickers to the shadows on the numbered doors to find out what object they will see behind each door.

# Jingly Jigsaw Puzzle

Complete the jigsaw to see who is decorating the Christmas tree and find out what is sitting right at the top of it. When you know the answer, circle the object at the bottom of the page.

# Frosty Footprints

Who's left footprints in the snow today? Follow the footprints to match the toys to their bunny owners and then add the correct stickers.

# Christmas Dot-to-Dot

Peter has made his very own snow character. What is it?
Join the dots to find out! Then stick on a nose, buttons,
eyes and a mouth. Don't forget to add arms!

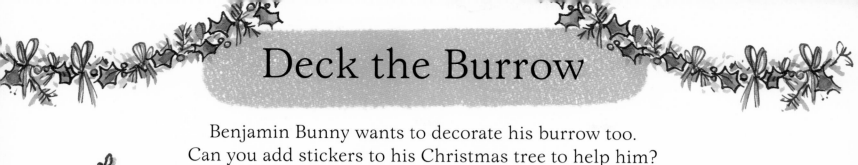

# Deck the Burrow

Benjamin Bunny wants to decorate his burrow too.
Can you add stickers to his Christmas tree to help him?

# A Letter for Father Christmas

Peter's writing to Father Christmas. Why don't you send a letter too? Complete the one below by drawing or writing your answers. Then, using your stickers, add lots of toys to Father Christmas's sack.

Dear Father Christmas,

I have been very good this year.

I would like

.........................................................................

.........................................................................

.........................................................................

for Christmas.

Love from,

.........................................

# Festive Patterns

Look at these rows of Christmas objects.
Use your stickers to complete each pattern.

# Cosy Clothes

Peter and Benjamin are off out to post Peter's letter to Santa.
Use your stickers to dress them in some warm winter clothes.

# A Misty Maze

Peter and Benjamin are on their way to the letterbox but a mist has set in and now they are lost. Can you help them find their way? Add some friendly woodland characters for the bunnies to meet through the woods.

*Title page*

*Peter's Advent Calendar*

*A Snowy Sticker Scene*

*Jingly Jigsaw Puzzle*

*Frosty Footprints*

*Christmas Dot-to-Dot*

*Deck the Burrow*

A Letter for Santa

Festive Patterns

A Misty Maze

Cosy Clothes

Christmas Eve

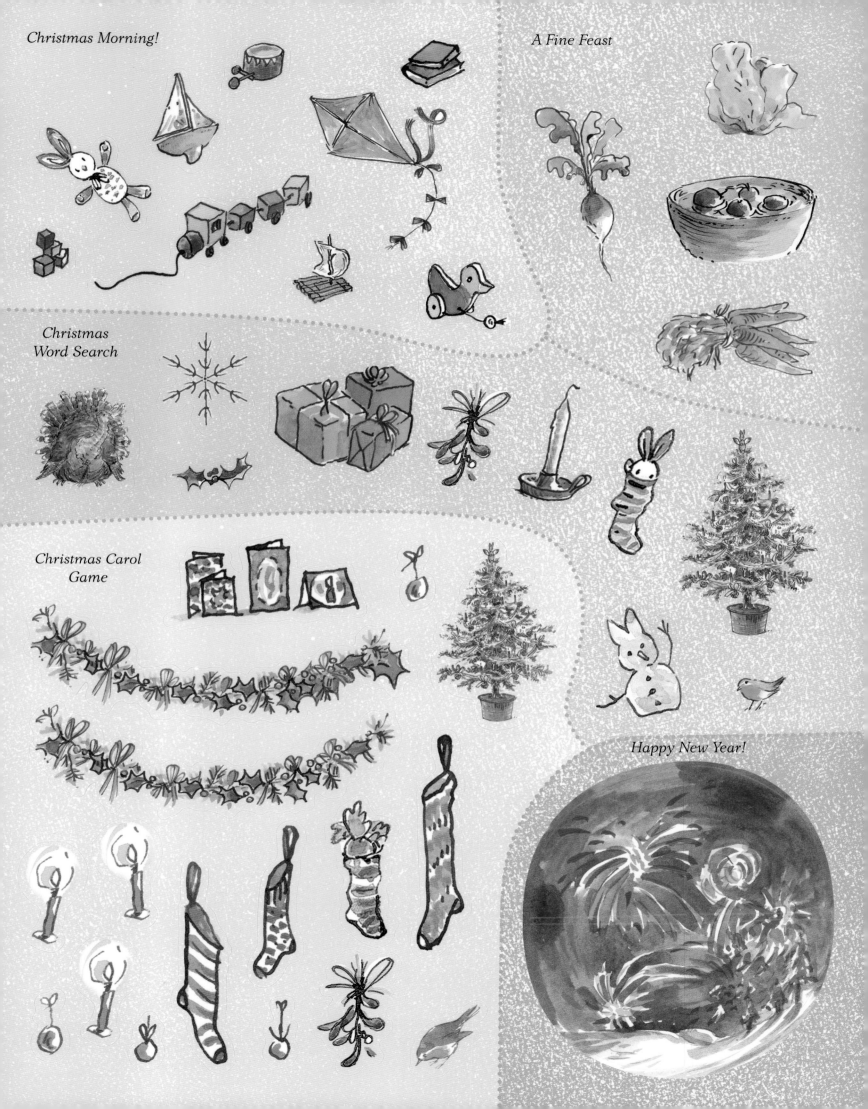

Christmas Morning!

A Fine Feast

Christmas
Word Search

Christmas Carol
Game

Happy New Year!

# Christmas Eve

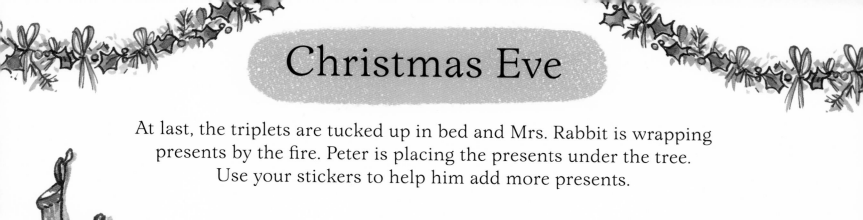

At last, the triplets are tucked up in bed and Mrs. Rabbit is wrapping
presents by the fire. Peter is placing the presents under the tree.
Use your stickers to help him add more presents.

# Spot the Difference

Peter was determined to stay awake to see Father Christmas but he's fallen asleep under the tree. There are six differences to find between these two pictures. Circle every difference you can find.

# Christmas Morning!

Santa's been! Peter and his sisters are busy opening their presents but they've made a bit of a mess! Can you help Mrs. Rabbit find all the toys in the burrow? Add a sticker of each toy that you find.

**RABBIT**

**KITE**

**SAILING BOAT**

**TRAIN**

**BOOKS**

**DRUM**

**BRICKS**

**DUCK**

**BOAT**

# Lace Up and Skate!

The pond has frozen over and all the animals have gathered for a Christmas skate.
Add your favourite characters to this festive skating scene.

# A Fine Feast

Peter and his sisters are looking forward to a tasty Christmas feast.
Add the stickers to match each rabbit's description.

### PETER
My favourite Christmas treat is pink
and crunchy with green leaves.

### FLOPSY
I love eating crunchy orange
vegetables at Christmas.

### MOPSY
Sweet and red, these fruity treats
are perfect for a festive feast.

### COTTON-TAIL
Leafy and green, these
are my favourites.

# Christmas Word Search

It really has been a wonderful Christmas at the burrow.
Can you find these 10 Christmas items in the grid?
When you find a word, add the matching sticker.

**TREE**

**ROBIN**

**HOLLY**

**SNOW BUNNY**

| M | I | S | T | L | E | T | O | E | C |
| D | J | N | U | W | L | V | N | E | T |
| C | H | O | R | I | P | S | I | R | G |
| A | T | W | K | A | R | M | B | T | N |
| N | E | B | E | O | E | F | O | Y | I |
| D | R | U | Y | W | S | H | R | O | K |
| L | D | N | O | S | E | N | T | L | C |
| E | I | N | S | L | N | T | A | I | O |
| K | S | Y | C | H | T | R | I | S | T |
| H | O | L | L | Y | S | M | V | A | S |

**SNOW**

**CANDLE**

**STOCKING**　　　**MISTLETOE**　　　**TURKEY**　　　**PRESENTS**

# Christmas Carol Game

The rabbits decide to go out carol singing in the woods.
Play this game with your friends, then decorate
the board with Christmas stickers.

Start

1

2

You meet Jemima
Puddle-Duck and
stop to sing.
**MISS A GO.**

4

You find William
the turkey hiding
behind a toadstool.
Shhh!
**GO BACK
TWO STEPS.**

19

18

17

21

22

**YOU WILL NEED:**

A die
5 counters – you can use
a coin or a button!

Quick!
It's Mr. McGregor
looking for
William.
**HIDE AND MISS
A GO.**

24

25

You pop into Ginger
and Pickles to sing a
carol to the customers.
**GO BACK
THREE STEPS.**

Squirrel Nutkin joins in. **MISS A GO.**

8

6

9

5

10

11

### HOW TO PLAY:

The youngest player rolls the die first
and moves the correct number of places.
Take it in turns to roll the die and
follow the instructions on the stepping stones.
The first bunny back to the burrow is the winner!

Mrs. Tiggy-Winkle is asleep and won't be disturbed. **HOP FORWARD FOUR STEPS.**

16

You meet the ever-helpful Jeremy Fisher. You sing a song and to thank you, he helps you get across the frozen pond. **THROW THE DIE AGAIN.**

14

13

27

28

29

30

Finish

# Festive Friends

Peter is going to a festive party with all his friends, but he has lost the cake! Show him which path he should take to find it.

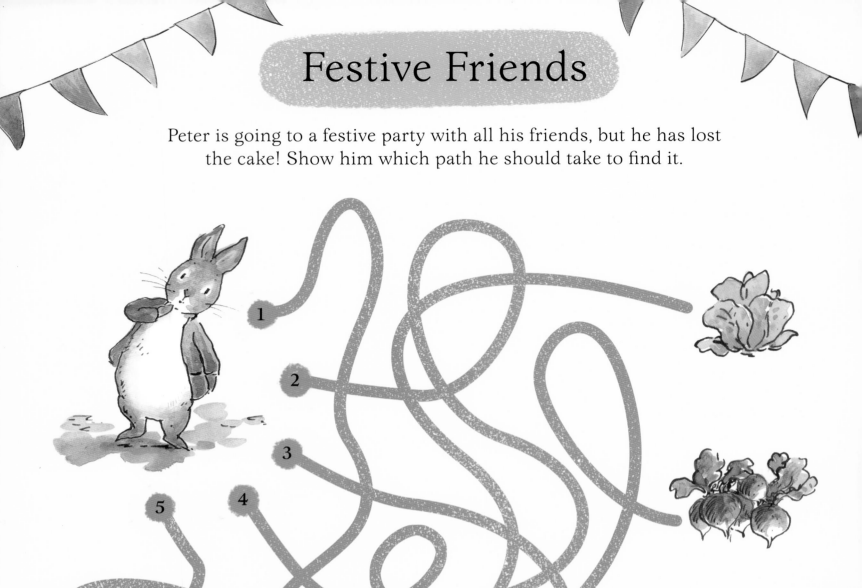

# Party Games

Peter's friends are all at the party. Draw a line to connect each friend with their shadow.

# Happy New Year!

Peter had a very happy Christmas. As he watches the New Year fireworks from his bedroom window, he says goodbye to another wonderful year with his family and friends. Use your stickers to add the bright and colourful fireworks.

## Answers

### Frosty Footprints

### Festive Patterns

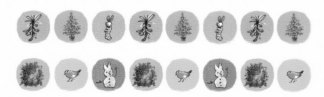

### A Misty Maze

### Spot the Difference

### Christmas Word Search

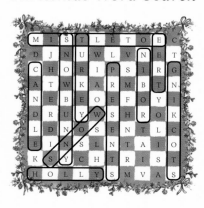

### Party Games

### Festive Friends

Peter should take path 3.